THERE'S SOMETHING IN MY ATTIC

written and illustrated by MERCER MAYER

Dial Books for Young Readers / New York

Published by Dial Books for Young Readers
A Division of NAL Penguin Inc.
2 Park Avenue
New York, New York 10016

Published simultaneously in Canada
by Fitzhenry & Whiteside Limited, Toronto

W
3 5 7 9 10 8 6 4 2

Library of Congress Cataloging in Publication Data

Mayer, Mercer, 1943–
There's something in my attic.

Summary: Convinced there is something making noise
in the attic at night, a brave little girl sneaks up the
stairs, lasso in hand, to capture whatever it is.
[1. Monsters—Fiction.] I. Title.
PZ7.M462Thd 1988   [E]   86-32875
ISBN 0-8037-0414-3
ISBN 0-8037-0415-1 (lib. bdg.)

*The art for each picture consists of pen, ink, and watercolor washes
that are color-separated and reproduced in full color.*

To Jessie, my daughter,
with love

Who was touched by Goopy
and went to Singapore?
Who had witches in the trees
and a finger on the door?
Who didn't like the thumber
or the lightning anymore?

I was never afraid of anything
when we lived in the city,
but now we live on a farm.

At night when the lights go out,
I get scared,

because I can hear

a nightmare in the attic

right above my head.

It doesn't seem to bother Mom and Dad.

They say it's probably mice.

But it sounds too big to be mice.

I decided to lasso that nightmare
and bring it down to show them.

I'd just be brave and sneak quietly
into the attic with my lasso ready.

It wasn't there.

But I noticed a bunch of toys

I thought were lost

lying in a pile behind some boxes.

Something weird was going on for sure.
Then I heard it creeping up the stairs.

"Hey," I called. "That's my teddy bear! Give it to me!"
But the nightmare tried to sneak back down the stairs.

So I chased it.

Then I lassoed it.
It was hugging my bear as hard as it could.

"Be careful, Nightmare," I said,
"or you'll rip my bear."

I tried to get my bear back,
but it wouldn't let go.

So I pulled it down the hall
to my parents' room.

I flipped on the lights

to show them the nightmare I captured.
I was sure they would be amazed.

But nightmares are very tricky, and sometimes they just slip away.

I'll just have to get my bear back tomorrow.